First published in Great Britain in 1999 by Madcap Books,
an imprint of André Deutsch Ltd,
76 Dean Street, London, W1V 5HA
www.vci.co.uk

Text and illustrations © 1999 Madcap Books

A catalogue record for this title is available
from the British Library

Design by Traffika Publishing
Reprographics by Modern Age Repro House Ltd

ISBN 0 233 99380 0

Printed in Italy by Officine Grafiche De Agostini

Answers to the puzzles

Page 10
Who is holding the hose? Freda has hose 1. Fred has hose 2. Fergus has hose 3.
Who's who under the car? Each mouse has a matching tail and whiskers.
Page 11
In Charlie's shop you will find: spades, string, scarfs, sweets, sunflowers, sunglasses,
slippers, shells, sausages, scales, seeds, strawberries and a ship in a bottle.
Page 21
Fishing. Tom catches the small fish; Tim catches the tin can; Matt catches the spotted fish;
Amanda catches the big fish; Dotty catches the long-lost umbrella.

Welcome to
MOUSE VILLAGE

GYLES BRANDRETH
illustrated by **MARY HALL**

MADCAP

Welcome to Mouse Village!

This is Matt Mouse. He is the village postmouse. Nobody knows Mouse Village better than Matt.

'Welcome to Mouse Village!' says Matt Mouse. 'You two must be the twins.'

'We are!' shout the twins.

'I'm Tim,' squeaks Tim.

'I'm Tom,' squeals Tom. 'We're staying with our Auntie.'

'I know your Aunt Myrtle. She runs the village teashop,' says Matt. 'She's got a slide in her garden. Can you see it on the map?'

'I can!' squeaks Tim. Can you? Can you see a maze and a pond, too?

If ever you get lost in Mouse Village, just look at the map and you will see where you are. And if you need a friend in Mouse Village, you've found him.

He's called Matt.

MOUSE VILLAGE

N
W E
S

station

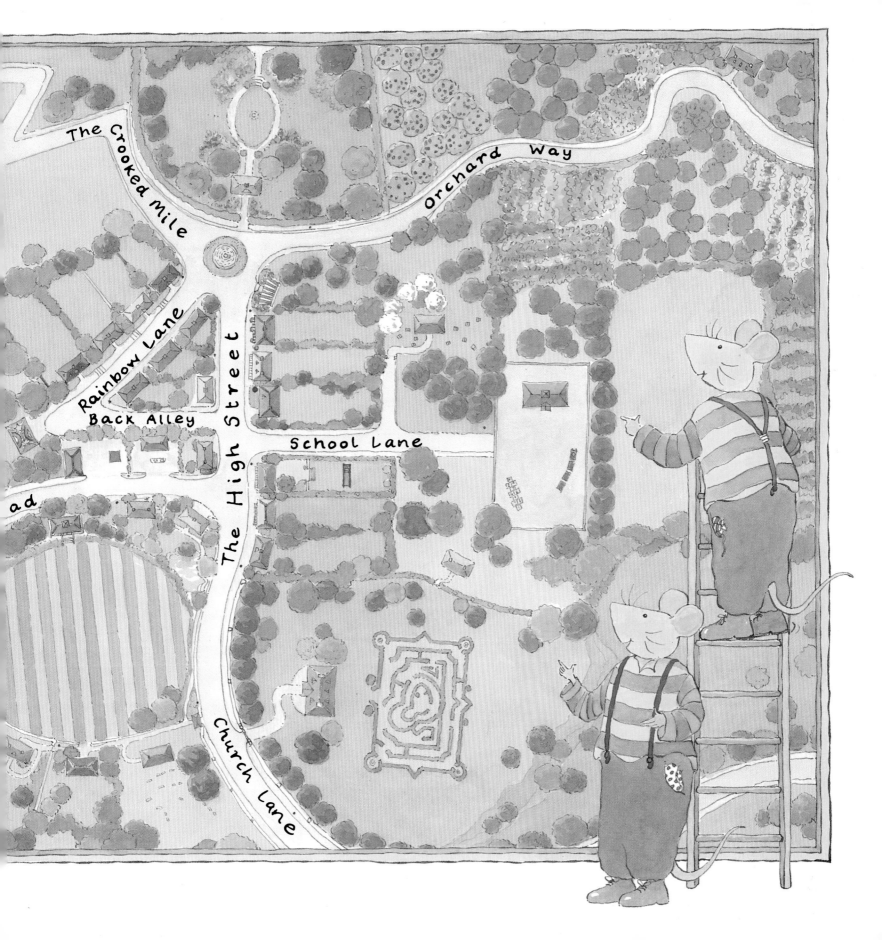

Every day Matt Mouse wakes up early.

He brushes his teeth.

And he washes behind his ears.

As the sun rises, he climbs on to his bike . . .

. . . and sets off for the Mouse Village
Railway Station,

in time to meet the first train.

There are always lots of letters and postcards
and parcels for the mice in Mouse Village.

Matt puts them in his bag
and off he goes.

He rides along Station Road towards the High Street
and cycles past the Mouse Village Fire Station.

The Mouse Village fire fighters are practising with their hoses.
Can you work out who is holding each hose?

As Matt rides past the Three Kind Mice Garage, he sees Beth and Bob and Bill
repairing Sir Hereward Mouse's car. By looking at their tails, Matt can tell
which mouse is which. Can you?

Matt stops at Charlie's Corner Shop. Matt has a letter for Charlie. Charlie has a question for Matt. 'I'm selling thirteen things that begin with the letter S. Can you spot them?' Can you?

Matt has something for everyone in the High Street. There's a parcel for Dotty Dormouse at the Dress Shop, and one for Mrs Sugar at The Sweet Shop. Matt also stops off at the Post Office because that's where he lives - and there's even a letter for him today!

There is a parcel for the Tea Shop, and something for Ben Mouse, the baker. There's even a parcel for Percival and Peregrine at 'Pots and Pans'. What a lot for Matt to carry!

'Thank you for my mail,' says Mrs Sugar. 'What sweet can I give you as a treat?'

'My favourite, please,' says Matt. Can you guess what Matt's favourite sweet is?

It's a little pink mouse, all made of sugar.

'Why is a sugar mouse always pink?' asks Matt as he nibbles its nose.

'Don't you know?' says Mrs Sugar, 'I thought every mouse knew that story.'

'Well,' says Mrs Sugar, 'Once upon a time, on top of Mouse Mountain, there lived a beautiful princess. Her name was Rose Pink and she was the loveliest mouse you ever saw.'

'Because Rose Pink was very beautiful - and very clever - and very rich - prince mice from around the world came to ask her to marry them.

'Every day for a year, she met a different prince. Do you know how many she met?'
'365,' says Matt.
'366,' says Mrs Sugar. 'It was a leap year.'

'And at the end of the year, she asked four mice to return. "I can't decide who I want to marry," she said. "So I will marry the prince who brings me the best present."

'The first prince gave Rose a piano. "I'm sorry, but I can't play the piano," she said. "You are not the right prince for me."

'The second prince gave a great green cactus. "Ouch! It's covered in prickles," said Rose. "I'm sorry, but you're not the prince for me."

'The third prince arrived with a golden crown on a cushion. The crown was far too big for Rose Pink's head. "I don't think you are the right prince for me," she said.

'Prince Charming was the last to arrive, bringing with him a little pink sugar mouse. "It's as sweet and as pretty as you are," he said. And Rose's mind was made up.

'So Princess Rose Pink and Prince Charming were married the very next day. And from that day, when two mice want to be

especially nice, they give each other a pink sugar mouse. And that, Matt, is why I'm giving this to you.'

When Matt has finished his sugar mouse, he delivers the rest of the mail before returning to Pots and Pans to see his friends, Percival and Peregrine. They have promised to show Matt what is in their parcel.

Wooden spoons!

'Percy wanted a drum set for his birthday,' explains Peregrine, 'But that's expensive, so I sent off for these. Look! We can pretend all our pots and pans are drums.'

'This is fun!' shouts Peregrine.

'This is noisy,' thinks Matt as he sets off to find Flora.

Flora's Flower Stall is at the far end of the High Street. Flora's flowers always look so lovely. Today she's got four bunches that are exactly the same.

Can you find them?

Matt buys a big sunflower to take to his friend, Bea Mouse. Bea lives down School Lane, in Honeypot Cottage.

'Hello, Bea. Why are you dressed like that?' asks Matt. 'I'm collecting honey and I don't want the bees to sting me by mistake.' 'How do bees make honey, Bea?'

'Some bees collect nectar from the flowers and turn it into a sticky mixture in their special honey stomachs.

'They fly back to the hive and pass the mixture to the honey-maker bees, who put it safely in a honeycomb inside the beehive.'

In the afternoon, Matt picks up the twins from outside Myrtle's Tea Shop and takes them on a special expedition to the four corners of Mouse Village.

At the village pond, they meet Amanda Mouse and Dotty Dormouse, and the five of them go fishing.

Who is going to catch what?

When they arrive at Mouse Hall, Sir Hereward Mouse wants to take
the twins to the middle of his amazing maze. Lady Harriet is waiting for them there.

Can *you* find your way to the middle of the maze?

When they go over to Jack's farm, Jack Mouse takes them into the orchard and asks the twins if they can spot the difference between his two apple trees.

There are fifteen differences in these two pictures. Can you spot them?

On their way to Bluebell Wood, Matt and the twins stop at the wishing well.
'Can we throw a button in?' asks Tim.

'No,' says Matt. 'The magic only works with a penny. I'll throw one into the well and my wish will come true. Watch . . .'

Suddenly, Magic Mouse appears. 'Hello, Tom. Hello, Tim,' he says.

'You look like a wizard!' cries Tom.
'He *is* a wizard,' laughs Matt.

'Were you hiding?' asks Tim. 'No,' says Magic. 'I was tying my shoelace.'

'I'm taking the twins to Bluebell Wood,' says Matt. 'Will you join us?'

'Of course,' says Magic. 'Magic things always happen there.' So they all set off along The Crooked Mile to Bluebell Wood.

'This is the perfect place to play hide-and-seek,' says Tom. 'You all go and hide and I'll stay here and count to ten.'

As Tom counts to ten, a strange figure can be seen running between the trees.

'It's a ghost!' squeals Tim.

'No, it isn't!' laughs Magic.

'I know who it is,' says Matt.

Do you?

'It's Ben Mouse, the baker, all covered in flour. He's coming to the Mouse Village picnic.'
'Hooray!' shout the twins. 'Everybody's here.'

Do you know who everyone is? You do? Well done. Welcome to Mouse Village.